MW01242749

The Broomstick
Christmas Tree

by
Jacqueline T. Moore

ALL RIGHTS RESERVED

Solstice Publishing -
http://www.solsticeempire.com/

I dedicate this book to my children Julie
Anne Jacobs and Nathan Robert James.

Chapter One

What have I gotten myself into? This can't be my life, sitting on a pot in a roadside gas station in west bumble who knows where, nursing an infant and wrangling a three year old. My grandmother would have an absolute fit if she knew.

"Mommy, Mommy, are we gonna see Mrs. Zippy? I wanna see Mrs. Zippy. And a cowboy. And go potty."

That last statement got my attention. I cricked my head around to the child behind me. "Sure, Punkin', can you hold it for just a little bit 'til we get to a gas station?"

"I gotta potty. Now." The 'now' was accompanied with a car seat pee-pee dance. "Now, now, now." She punctuated her words with pink-sneakered kicks, jingling the rattle trapeze bar closed up in the playpen stuffed behind the front seat. "Want dinosaur place."

Her daddy groaned, hollered "Quit kickin' my seat," and sped up, finding the closest Sinclair Oil station, the one with its dinosaur logo. That's the only gas charge card we ever qualified for. Pulling up to the pump, the lack of tire vibration woke baby Bobby. With eyes popped wide and mouth realizing nothing was in it, he announced he was awake and hungry. Miss 'gotta go' three-and-a-half-year-old pee-pee dancer, the ever-present stuffed monkey, Zippy, under her arm, vaulted out of the car. Slinging the diaper bag over my shoulder, I hoisted Mister 'nurse me now' four month old on my hip. With a half-used packet of food stamps shoved in my pocket, I headed to the only place where I could do it all. In a gas station stall somewhere in eastern Iowa the world's problems were solved. Annie made it on time while I landed on the throne, taking care of my own business. I both changed and nursed Bobby with my blue jeans around my ankles in that smelly but private restroom.

I remember when…

There had been much promise. We met first day on campus. Danny was my only college love, and we matched in all the right ways. Working like crazy, I finished school and was teaching at age twenty, just so we could graduate together and get married later on in that golden summer of Woodstock, free love, and dreams of world peace.

Did we graduate together? Nope. He surprised me and his family with the announcement that he was missing one important state required credit, Physical Education, for God's sake. He would have to stay on campus for six weeks to finish.

Did I go to Woodstock? Nope. I spent the summer living with my parents, teaching school. Mom bought me my first legal cocktail at my bridesmaids' luncheon, a frozen daiquiri, saying it was a proper ladies' drink. July twentieth found us all sitting in front of the TV watching Neil Armstrong, me addressing wedding invitations on an aluminum folding snack table.

Was there world peace? Nope. That bloody war in Vietnam raged on no matter how many hopefuls held hands, singing 'Kumbaya', 'Blowin' In the Wind', or 'Where Have All the Flowers Gone?' I knew all the words by heart. That didn't matter a whit for world peace.

We were married in my family church. Our wedding night had him champagne drunk, passed out on the motel's floor. We honeymooned in his grandmother's summer cabin, with her in attendance, telling us that it was OK with her if we wanted to take a bath together. Uh, no thank you.

Danny and I played well together until almost four years later when our little

Annie arrived right on schedule. I was teaching. He was self-employed. I loved our New York suburb. He was bored. We stopped playing. Dutifully I followed him to different locales as he tried to find work, me teaching in every city we landed. Finally, thanks to Grandmother's honeymoon cabin in the Smoky Mountains and both of us getting decent jobs, we conceived child number two. One whole month later Danny got fired.

And look where I am now, for God's sake. Drawing unemployment and fighting the bureaucracy for assistance. That kind of stuff was never presented in Better Homes and Gardens or even Family Circle.

Tearing the correct amount of stamps from the packet, I bought two tins of Armour Vienna Sausages, a box of Sealtest Saltines, a pint of chocolate milk, and two Cokes. I splurged on a Pay Day candy bar. That peanut-covered caramel glob of goodness was the first pay day we'd seen in quite a while. Danny helped by standing near the car, talking conspiringly with the pump jockey. I saw them shake hands. The gas guy winked and stuffed his pocket. My husband handed over the charge card with a return wink, and looked at me. "You guys make it on time?"

I side-eyed the grinning pump kid. Turning my back on him, I replied, "Yep, How about you two? Get it done?" He nodded. Holding up the paper sack, I said, "Here, you take the baby, Annie and I are gonna set up lunch and look at the map."

Annie was our official cartographer. Her eyes flashed. "Can I make the line? I wanna use the fat red crayon."

"Of course, I'll show you where we are now." I spread the free Triple A map on the car hood. Our goal was to make it from western North Carolina to central Nebraska by nightfall, an impossible goal that included no motels.

Annie scrambled up on the front bumper. Standing on tip-toe, she stretched to see over the hood. "Show me, Mommy." She hoisted the monkey. "Zippy wants to see, too."

With one arm around her tiny back, holding her in place, I guessed, pointing to a spot about an inch and a half from the last crayon mark. "Start here and color to your last line."

She giggled. "Does Daddy have to drive backwards if I draw backwards?"

"Silly bump." I kissed her blond head. *Oh, dear Lord, help me do this. This trip is way too long for little ones...and their mommy.*

"We're heading forwards, no matter what," I assured her.

"Is this where we're goin'?" She pointed to my black circle around Grand Island. "Are we gonna stop there? At Nebasky" She poked the map. "Zippy's getting sleepy."

"I hope so. We're planning on it. Daddy and I are getting tired, too."

There, mid Nebraska, a college friend's couch waited for us to crash. After all, what else should we be doing in the middle of wintry November with two kids, a man with the shortest career on record, food stamps, and one of my first unemployment checks after being caught in a "Reduction in Force'? Why, of course, this RIF, a glorified lay off thanks to the district not passing a school tax, was perfect timing for traveling across country to Colorado for a brothers' Thanksgiving. All this made perfect sense…in *his* mind.

I looked at her. "Hungry?"

"Uh huh. Teeny weenies and cackas?"

"No baby talk. Crackers."

"And cho-co-late milk," she enunciated, grinning.

The Nebraska buddy's place was waiting, offering two days of food and rest. We thanked him with our usual trades. And then, westward ho. Annie saw the Mississippi and cried for miles when she realized that it wasn't the mate of her beloved stuffed monkey. "Mommy, it's a river." She was inconsolable. Her sobs escalated. "It's a river. You said it was Missus Zippy. I want to see a mommy monkey."

"Sweetheart, pretend Wife's your mommy monkey." I twisted in my seat to look at her. The trip was wearing on our nerves. "Just make believe."

"Yes, for God's sake, just pretend," snapped her daddy.

"Wife is my dolly, not an animal." *Annie sure did know her species.*

"Please. You can change Wife's name. How about calling her Mommy Monkey?" I could just about see her brain gears turning.

"Well, ok." She held the two to face each other. "Zippy, this is your mommy. Wife, this is your baby." The toys hugged. Annie giggled. "A people mommy and a monkey baby, that's silly."

"Baby, you are my little monkey."

"I thought I was your Punkin'."

I yawned. "Well, I guess you're my Punkin' Monkey. Now hush."

"Punkin' Monkey, Punkin' Monkey, Punkin' Monkey." she started chanting, bouncing in her seat to the rhythm of the road.

"You hush. Now." His tone was harsh and she got the message.

Two days, several weed and food stamp barters later, we rolled into Colorado, landing at Russell's, the oldest brother's house. I'd never seen a neighborhood like this. The streets had wide concrete ditches on each side. There were no lawns, no flowers, absolutely nothing growing. Yards were filled with small, round stones, some spray-painted green. One sported a painted stone sunburst, another, a black rock peace sign. Russel's dirt yard was full of bikes and kids' stuff. Two hitched camping trailers, parked side by side in the driveway, announced that we were the last to arrive. We pulled in behind the blue Shasta we recognized as belonging to Johnny, the youngest brother. The other camper was green, with tell-tale Airflyte wings on the sides. We'd never seen that one before. Up went the garage door, there was Russell standing with the biggest grin, waiting for us.

"Get yourselves in here, y'all. We've got the party started."

Danny was quick out of the car, doing the "Hey man, missed you" handshake and hug that men do when they don't want to be considered too girly. "Good to see ya, man. Where's the rest of the crew? I see Johnny's trailer. Did you guys break down and buy a Flyte, too?"

"Naw, not big enough for us 'n' two kids." He grinned. "The green one's Johnny's girl's. She's a pistol." He came to my side of the car, sticking his head in the window. "Hey, Miss Sister, you're lookin' good."

I smiled. "You, too."

"Wanna see my monkey?" Annie was practically climbing out the window. "His name is Zippy. He's got a people mommy."

"He does?" Russell pulled monkey and child out of the car, giving both a big hug. Pointing them to the door on the far wall, he said, "Why don't you show Zippy to everybody? They're in the kitchen." He turned to us. "Give me that boy and let's get you two a brew. Lulu'll want to show ya the house."

"How 'bout showing me the facilities first." Danny raised an eyebrow. "Gotta take a leak. Been on the road forever since the last gas station."

This brother and his wife, Loretta, called Lulu, had two little ones a bit older than ours. As we got the grand tour, I noticed the children's room had no bedding at all, just sleeping bags and pillows on stained slabs of foam rubber. I also noticed that Lulu wasn't embarrassed.

Our Colorado guest room was the heated garage with a mismatching box spring and mattress on the floor, no bedstead. At least it had a bottom sheet and an old quilt. While everyone else was in the kitchen drinking, talking, and kid admiring, I was fixing up the playpen in the garage. I put it close by the mattress so I could see Annie sleeping. I didn't need to worry about the baby. He practically lived in his car seat.

"Hey, girl, come get a cold one."

"I'm comin', I'm comin'."

I found Bobby perched on the table in the breakfast nook, looking like a wise ol' Buddha, watching the goings on. Crossing my fingers, I hoped his daddy had kept the safety strap across his wiggly tummy. The Colorado cousins had already commandeered Annie into cartoon watching in the living room.

"Hey, kids, turn that TV down," yelled Russell. "We can't hear ourselves think."

"Yeah," echoed their mother. "Turn that damned thing down."

The case of Coors was half gone by the time I pulled the pop top on my own. That was one good beer. Seems Johnny, youngest of the litter, had just rolled in with Dee Dee, his woman of the week. They were traveling separately, towing their own rigs.

"We found each other at a Kansas road side park." Dee Dee did a little shoulder shimmy shake. "He was coming out of the outhouse. I was next in line. I told him his barn door was open."

Johnny shrugged. "I told her the horse wanted out. I guess she liked the cowboy, too."

"I think he just wanted to see the inside of my Flyte." Dee Dee snorted. "We stayed parked, rockin' and rollin' until Smokey banged on the side, hollerin' at us to move along. Johnny told me about this shindig, so I decided to check it out." She shrugged. "And here I am in my Green Machine."

We women sat around the table, not talking much, watching the brothers sitting at the breakfast bar, getting reacquainted. Their conversations led almost directly to boyhood antics and memories of mischief. After a bit, male voices became background noise as ignored females in that room hadn't any inkling as to what they were talking about. The guys were too deep in their reunion to fill us in.

Lulu was absently making a chain of all the beer pulls, looping each tab through the last ring. She gestured with her head. "Gonna add them to the door." The pantry shelves had rows of thumbtacked pop tops hanging like hippy beads. "Plan to do every door that way. They jingle and shine. Don't ya think it's classy?" She pointed to the kitchen window with pride. "And I made those curtains out of the kids' top sheets. Just run a rod through the sewed part, and," snapping her fingers, "there ya go. Cut 'em off to fit after I put 'em up." Lulu opened another Coors and chugged it. "Hey, guys," she said loud enough to get the brothers' attention. "Don't throw away your pop tops. I'm making curtains with them. See." She added her top to the chain.

"Yeah, she's one high class interior decorator." Her husband turned to the table, sarcasm dripping. "We're livin' in a real mansion. That's why we always have the guys here on weekends, uh never."

"Shut up, Russ, I'm decoratin' this place good. You and your high falutin' buddies can just keep goin' to the O club on base." Lulu turned to me, eyes pleading, "Y'all love 'em, don'tcha?"

"I've never seen anything like it," I replied truthfully, jiggling the silver strip, spilling the tabs from hand to hand. "That takes a lot of pop tops. Did you think this up yourself?"

"Yep." She looked at the metal pantry curtain. "He thinks we should be livin' in officer's quarters with all those stuck up bitches. Hah, not me."

"Yeah, I thought I married her for better, but now it's mostly worse." He turned back to the breakfast bar and the beers.

Lulu lowered her eyes, looking at her shiny stash of rings. "Been savin' 'em for a while now," she whispered to no one in particular. After a bit she looked at me, eyes glistening, "Want me to start saving you some? I can fill ya a Mason jar in no time. We drink a lot of beer."

"Um, no thanks, Bobby might, er, swallow one."

Dee Dee shook her head. "Me neither. My rig's got built-in blinds."

The brothers, each a few years apart, had been a tight-knit pack up until high school. Then Vietnam happened. The oldest became a super-duper somethin' or other Air Force lifer, a top rank NCO here in Colorado. My husband was declared 4F, having been 'sort of' diagnosed with a possible rare disease, and the youngest one was just out of his shortened time in the Force, narrowly escaping a rumored stint in a third world jail. Nobody saw combat and this was their first time together since the youngest was discharged. They immediately became twelve again, only this time insanely drunk.

The table fell silent as the men decided to step out back to "water the rocks." I was beyond exhausted, but felt the need to try making conversation.

"Um, Lulu, how is the school system in this neighborhood?" Education was something I could talk about. Her kids were almost old enough to start.

She stared at me. "Huh?"

"You know, the school where your kids will go?" Looking at her blank face, I had the feeling she's never thought about it before.

"Um, I don't know *how* it is, but as long as it's close enough for them to walk, I don't care." Stubbing out her cigarette, she shrugged, "Never learned to drive. Not gonna, don't wanna."

"Oh." Not one to give up, I turned to Dee Dee. "Speaking of education, do you have any children?"

"Hell, no rug-rats for me. Like my rig life too much." Pointing toward the front door, she added, "Guess that Green Machine's my bundle of joy."

Silence prevailed until the 'rock waterers' returned for a refill and to fetch the starter fluid to fire up the briquettes in the grill.

"Um, why are there rocks in everybody's yards? And what are the ditches for?" I was sincerely curious. *Maybe, just maybe, this could start a conversation.*

Lulu shrugged. "Too much altitude. Good for a Rocky Mountain high, but not for growin' grass. The ditches are for storms, 'cause when it rains, it pours." She giggled. "I saw that on a Morton Salt box."

"Such an idiot, a real loony loo loo," muttered her husband. Lulu flinched.

"My real name's Loretta," she mouthed silently.

He looked at his wife and with a head yank toward the back door, barked, "Bring the burgers when I holler. Don't forget the salt and pepper like last time." He whistled a shrill bobwhite. His two, with Annie in hand, came running. "Come on, kids, let's make some noise."

"Can we shoot fire crackers?" asked his five-year-old.

"Yep."

"Woohoo!"

I looked at Lulu. "You let them play with fire?"

"Sure, they ain't too young to learn. My daddy always said the best way to not burn yourself is to burn yourself." She held up her right hand, pointing to her pinky. "See that scar? 'Bout blew my finger off. That was the best bottle rocket lesson I ever learned."

"Oh, my," was my quiet response. *Oh, God, how did I get here?*

Out they went again, Annie, following the lead of her cousins, making 'bang bang' sounds and flying her hands in the air like the Fourth of July fireworks we watched this past summer.

That night, finally settled under the quilt, Danny snoring beside me, I realized why there was such prickliness around that kitchen table. The women were afraid to step on the egg shells that represented the relationships we each had. In the eyes and words of the sons' parents, I was the educated, proper one and could do no wrong, and they let everyone know it.

Loretta was a stray mangy mutt their beloved first born brought into the family without announcement, thought to lifestyle, or breeding. The folks didn't like this disappointment one bit. Johnny was the baby and pretty much got away with whatever he wanted. With his history of many girlfriends, Dee Dee didn't pose a threat because they didn't know.

As the week wore on, I noticed the brothers were continually and familiarly behaving badly toward their women. Through the years I thought I was the only one. However, all three women were coldly ignored, condescended to with cutting sarcasm, or curtly ordered to serve them. We were generally disrespected in a way that the guys considered normal. No one spoke up.

One afternoon the men decided to go out, probably on a beer run, taking Russell's kids with them. While I stayed in the garage with napping babies, Lulu and Dee Dee joined me on the communal mattress, six packs in tow. Bobby was zonked in his seat and Annie and Zippy were curled up in the playpen.

Free from the fear of her husband's criticism, Lulu grabbed an ashtray, pulled out her Benson Hedges Menthols, and spoke. "Um, Susan, can I ask you a question?"

"Sure," I said hopefully. "What is it?"

"It's about our mother- in- law."

"OK. What do you want to know?"

"Well I've only met her once, and she was polite and all, but…" she hesitated.

"But what?" I popped my own beer and handed her the top.

"Is she always so quiet, doin' what she's told?"

I answered that I had never heard her make a peep about anything,

"Well then, is Dad always so bossy? He made me real nervous that time we visited." Taking a drag on her cig and a swig from her beer, she lifted her smoke. "He treated me like I was some sort of trailer trash nothin' for smoking."

I rolled my eyes. "He told me I must be Catholic because I have pierced ears."

"What?" They reacted in unison.

"Yep, he said I must be Catholic because all Mexicans have pierced ears and they are Catholic, so I must be, too." I grimaced. "What an ass." Lulu and I looked at each other. I shook my head. "Did you know Mom has to sneak to watch television?"

"Did you know he won't let anyone use bath towels? You gotta dry with a wash cloth like they taught him in the war." Lulu took another swig. "He told me that the one time we visited. Russell tried that crap on me. No way!"

"Yeah, but Mom has to wash and iron cloth napkins for the dinner table. Hasn't she ever seen the commercial for Manners the Butler and his Kleenex napkins?"

Dee Dee chimed in. "How would she? She's not allowed to watch TV, for

God's sake." That brought a beer can cheer as we all clunked our Coors and drank.

Dee Dee shared that the family didn't know about her and that was all right. "I'm already sick and tired of Johnny cuttin' his eyes at me like I'm some sorta moron for not reading his mind and handing him his freakin' heart's desire without him saying what it is." She stood, stretched and started pacing the garage. "I've had it, being treated like I'm invisible and utterly stupid at the same time. Planning to get me and my rig outta here as soon as Turkey Day is done. Can't take the crap he's pullin'. Don't have to. This week has been long enough." Shaking her head, she got to the heart of the matter. "Too bad for you guys, though, you're stuck. I can split. Not so easy with kids."

Finishing each other's sentences, we broke the silent barriers of pride and loyalty that shrouded our lonely lives. Dee Dee could escape, the wives were stuck. I didn't know about Lulu, but I knew that my wedding vows and the responsibilities they represented were crushing me. My marriage was no partnership.

That conversation created the rest of my life. *Oh my God, it's not me. I did not cause this.* The brothers were acting just like their father, behaving toward women the way they were taught. It was all they knew. Privately giving us two years for me to fix us, I now knew that I could not fix anything. This miserable life was not my fault. For our entire time together I taught school, paid the bills, and parented those two wonderful children, all the while feeling the guilt of the failure. If only I would do more, be skinnier, act nicer, make more money to counter his chronic lack of employment, maybe then he would hug me. Or hold the children on a regular basis. Or be ambitious about something, anything. If only he hadn't smoked dope on the only decent job he ever had the month we bought our first new piece of furniture, the month I thought I was finally safe, the month we knew a baby was on the way. *If only...*

That day in that garage I knew I must leave, that I had to escape to save me and the children. And I did.

Chapter Two

Christmas week was hell.

The long, exhausting car ride cross country, back to North Carolina, gave me the courage to think the unthinkable and plan the unforgivable. He wasn't chatting, and I was totally into mommy mode. The kid's car naps allowed my internal dialogue to run wild.

Gotta leave. Gonna be ok. Yeah, right. Maybe I should take the kids and run away to Hollywood, become a movie star and get rich. Naw. How about the circus? I can see the headlines now. SINGLE MOTHER OF TWO JUGGLES CHILDREN WHILE STILL WEARING WHITE CHURCH GLOVES. Nope, I told myself, *"The circus isn't the answer. Too smelly. I'll get a teaching job. Yep, school's for me.*

That next week brought 'the talk'. The kids were sleeping, so I went looking for Danny, finding him at the bottom of the driveway hill in the old barn that was once our chicken coop. Lice and foxes killed them all. After that horrible week of blood covered feathers, I never went near the place again, still afraid there'd be critters lurking. However, this day, I got brave. He was messing with his latest project, something about selling reclaimed wood to snow birds and making a bundle.

Struggling to get the words out, I stammered, "Danny, I can't do this."

"Huh?" He looked up from his pile of rotting treasures.

"I can't live like this; not here, not with you, not anymore."

"Huh? What do you mean?" He picked up a barn plank and eyed it like he really had a clue what he was doing. "Ya think this is too warped to sell."

"Did you hear what I just said?"

He shrugged. "Not really." Setting down the board, he pulled out his smokes. "What are you talking about?"

Tears started. "I am done, done with you, done with us."

His face went from puzzled to pissed. "You can't be done. We got kids."

"And?"

"And, and," he sputtered, "And, well you can't just leave them. I don't know how to take care of them. They'll get hungry, or something. And you know about the water."

"Oh, my God, you idiot, don't worry. I'm taking them with me." If nothing else gave me courage, his last statement sealed the deal. Voice rising, I let it all out. "These past six years of being the only steady paycheck, the responsible one, the provider of all, made me realize there has to be one less mouth to feed, and it is yours!"

"Whatever." He went back to his prized piece of crap, er, board.

A separation date for January was set and it was decided that we would not tell anyone until we were into the next year. I guess he was as miserable as I was, but he never expressed himself enough to let me know. He just stayed high.

Soon the holidays had us driving again, this time north to my folks' newly-purchased forever home. This would be Bobby's first peek at Santa and Annie's first real-believing Christmas, snow and all. Mom and Dad's house was not my home and, with dread, we followed the written directions to a strange suburb I only knew by name.

We were met at the door by glowing grandparents. Mom, arms extended, did her 'give me that baby' finger wiggle dance, snatching Bobby. "Child, look at you. I've not seen you since you were born," she cooed, kissing him all over his fuzzy little head. "You're sooo big."

"Give me that Little Missy." Daddy looked Annie square in the eyes. "Can I call you that?"

"Uh huh, Pop Pop, but you're the only one allowed to. OK?"

"Deal." Daddy carried his Little Missy and Zippy, singing 'Jingle Bells', bouncing her in his arms in time to the song. That left me to lug in the ever-present playpen. The four of us were squeezed in the guest room. My empty-handed husband found the couch, using his 'maybe diagnosis' to not lift a finger. He watched the activities through a cigarette haze as I unloaded the car, hauling in the suitcases, trying hard not to let the folks see my weariness.

That night, after the kids were asleep, my parents asked us into the living room. Standing by a glowing tree, we were each handed a glass of champagne. Mom was beaming. "We've waited since last summer to share this with you two."

"Oh?" *Last summer, what happened last summer?*

"Yes siree," Daddy piped up. "Our anniversary's in August, but we waited because we wanted you guys to witness our thirty-year vow renewal. We're going to have a little wedding right here, right now."

Oh, dear God.

Holding hands, faces lit by the flicker of bubble lights and garlands, they spoke:

"I love and will continue to love you. Tonight we start the rest of our lives."

"I love and will continue to love you. Tonight we start the rest of our lives."

Daddy slipped a new diamond band on Mom's left ring finger, took her in his arms, and kissed her, I almost threw up.

By Christmas Eve there was no hiding our mess. The misery was undeniable, practically palatable. Danny and I were barely talking, passing each other in that strange house like dark thunderheads in a sky of red and green tinsel. The forced conversations around the dinner were especially horrid. I made sure the attention was on the kids and their antics. Half the time Danny didn't come to the table, claiming leg weakness from his maybe disease, and asked that I bring him a plate to the couch.

The family went to candle light services at Concord, my childhood church where I grew up, where I sang in the choir as a teen, where we got married. Each congregant received a white candle, and when the time came, the flame was passed from wick to wick. I cried through three stanzas of Silent Night, my flame trembling in the darkness.

Back at the house, Mom pulled me into their bedroom, shaking her head. "Whatever is going on between you and Danny is really getting on our nerves." She sighed. "You guys need to talk. We think you should go somewhere and work out whatever this is. Daddy says a beer always helps. Coming home from church, I noticed the Maple Grove is open."

"But, it's…"

"We'll put the kids to bed. Go talk."

Good God Almighty, a bar, on Christmas Eve… to talk? Bars charged money we didn't have, and we didn't want to talk.

She smiled. "We'll pull Santa duty. It's been a long time since we've filled stockings." She hugged me tight. "Now, shoo. Get this worked out. Don't ruin Christmas."

We sat at a high top in a dark corner next to the silent pool table. Someone had punched up 'I'll Be Home for Christmas' on the jukebox. *Oh, goody, just what I need, a seriously sad song.* Looking at Danny, I whispered "Damn thing's too loud."

"What'd ya say?"

Swiveling to my left, I looked straight into the eyes of one of the shortest, skinniest man I'd seen in a long time. I couldn't help but stare his wispy comb over grown long enough to connect with a ponytail, hanging down his back. He looked like an old wannabe biker guy. "Music's too loud."

"Easy fix. Be back in a jiff." And he was. I noticed his bar apron went around him twice, tied in the front with a double knot. "Well, little lady, is that better?"

I nodded, wishing it would just turn off; praying Bing Crosby's 'White Christmas' wasn't next.

"Name's Tom, what can I get you two?" The bar-keep stood on tip-toe to swipe his rag across some crusted ketchup spilled in front of me. The glob didn't move.

Danny lit a Camel. "What's your cheapest beer?"

"Pabst. You each want one?"

Nodding, I finally took in that gloomy place. Our companions for the evening included one very drunk, raccoon eyed, bleached blond woman chain-smoking cigarettes and talking loudly to the chain-smoking blond in the mirror behind the bar. They both were wearing a red sweater with silver threads woven through the appliqued tree resting square on their bosom. Add a scattering of souls, including one very confused man in a disheveled green elf suit, his orange Leprechaun beard slid sideways so that he could drink. Two guys in faded fatigues, evidently war casualties no hospital could fix, were arguing. I caught words like "traitor', 'Jane Fonda', and 'commie bitch.' With no obvious place to be, this very sad holiday party was complete, and somehow, a young couple ending their marriage on Christmas Eve just fit in. One PBR later we drove back to my parents' house. There had been no talking.

Christmas morning started with a fancy breakfast at home, including Mom's traditional cinnamon strudel coffeecake. Daddy gave me his 'watch this' eyebrow lift and gathered Annie to his lap. On his breakfast plate was a dinner knife and a giant glob of margarine, his favorite topping for any sugary sweet.

"Tell me, Little Missy, are you allowed to use a knife?"

"Uh uh, I'm too little. Mommy says knives are 'danger danger'." She looked at me, waiting for the safety alarm I practically shouted to scare her away from anything she might hurt herself with.

I kept quiet.

Well then, are you allowed to drink coffee?" Her Pop Pop picked up his usual concoction of four spoons of sugar and enough milk to disguise the bitterness and made a loud slurp.

Annie shook her head. "No coffee. Yucky for kids."

"What if I told you that this is not coffee. What if I told you that this is called café au lait, and it's a fancy drink just for little girls and their Pop Pops."

She looked at me. "OK, Mommy?" I smiled and nodded, knowing where this was headed.

That morning Annie was introduced to butter smearing, coffee cake dunking, and what became her favorite beverage. I joined in with my own cup, spooning buttery cinnamon strudel out of creamy 'French Coffee'.

Celebrations with two different sets of great grandparents, one for lunch, one for dinner, filled the day. The kids were the center of attention with each set vying to outdo each other with gigantic spreads of food and presents galore. No one noticed that not one word or gift was exchanged between the children's parents.

The day after Christmas, we headed south. Once we were settled into that cabin with no insulation and only a central oil burning heater, I called. The polite explanation to my family was that, after him not maintaining employment for our entire marriage, all of it was my fault because I'd run out of wifely patience. I just couldn't take it anymore. That was how the separation was announced. I didn't tell my parents about the coldness, the sarcasm, the deep loneliness of his refusal to touch me or play with the children, and the fact that the water line running from the spring high up the mountain to the uninsulated log cabin we lived in was frozen solid and that he had to pull water from a nineteenth century well out back.

Who knows what he told his folks.

Chapter Three

The second week in January I moved me and my kids five miles away into a furnished monthly-rental two bedroom mobile home. I brought my oak rocking chair, clothes for everyone, and little else. The trailer had running water, heat, and thin but real walls, all improvements from what I was used to. I took the master and made a sort of safe bed for my kids, laying them together across the double in the guest room. I surrounded them with the crib bumpers as a soft reminder not to fall out of bed. It sort of worked. Nobody hit the floor, but one morning I did find Bobby hanging feet first over the edge.

During the three months we lived in the trailer, I'd been called to do a lot of substitute teaching. It paid my bills, including the same babysitter I used before the lay-off. Danny replaced me with an electric pasture fence in the front field and a steer to slaughter. I never touched the animal or the fence. I figured he traded one cash cow for another.

The plan was to go to free marriage counseling offered by graduate students at the local college. Friends close by kept the kids, hoping we could work things out. My husband's continued sarcasm and biting negativity in front of the psychologist quickly led to individual sessions. For three months we attended weekly "shrink night", as he called it, with no change between us. My therapist carefully guided me to understand that sometimes vows must be broken, giving me the strength to save the children and myself.

We had no assets since I insisted the Corolla be in my name. After all, I was making the payments. He agreed to marital dissolution, a divorce for poor people. One day I stopped by the cabin to pick up some more clothes for the kids when he asked me to get out the wedding gift scrap book with the thank-you list. He insisted we split our stuff down the middle. "You get four plates, I get four plates. You get half the spoons, forks, and knives." He pointed to the kitchen cupboard. "Get out the pots and pans. I get half."

"Why? You don't cook. You can't even sweep a floor." I started stacking the cast iron skillets and Revere Ware set.

"Give me half, dammit, they're mine." His tone unnerved me.

I cursed back and hurled the smallest Revere Ware sauce pan, hoping to hit him upside the head with its copper bottom. Missed him, dented the pan. He kept it anyway.

Mid-April I called, asking my parents if I could come home. Mom said "Of course". Dad said "We don't get divorces in this family. What do you want from me? It's your bed, you made it, you lay in it." I heard Mom screaming at him in the background as I slammed down the phone. Finally, I cried. It took two days but he called back, begging forgiveness, assuring me that he would be there soon. I started packing what we had in the trailer.

My father brought his pick-up to that rugged cabin, the site of my heart-break. "Well, with your mom still teaching at Patterson Elementary, it sure is lucky I got my retirement. We moved the TV to the living room and changed the den into the kids' room. Put in a crib and everything. You get the guest room. You mother has everything set up, and I got my old wooden high chair out of the attic." Dad finally smiled. "That boy of ours is big enough to fit where I used to sit." He side hugged me. "Meet your new nanny, er, grampy."

I rolled into my daddy's arms, feeling true safety for the first time in what seemed like an eternity.

Danny finally held his children as Dad and I loaded the pickup to haul everything I owned back to Dayton, back to where I started. There was my beloved piano, rocking chair, and the heirloom four-poster bed made by my grandpa in high school woodworking shop. I took the couch and matching chair I paid for the week before Danny was fired. Adding in our clothes and box after box of the wedding gifts he carefully divided, no matter that he was one and I was a family of three, Dad's truck was full.

"Oh, did I tell you we rented you a storage bin down on County Line Road by the old house? Mom and I paid three months; the rest is up to you." He grinned. "We know things will be looking up by then."

"Oh, Daddy, I sure hope so." I started singing what I remembered of the fifty's hit. "Sha na na na,sha na na na na, get a job."

He smiled, "You can do it, kiddo, I know you can."

While Daddy was strapping my bicycle to the back of the Toyota, Danny asked me to come into the cabin. Together one last time, he got out his guitar and sang Jimmy Buffett's "Margaritaville'. He stopped the song after the verse "Some people say there's a woman to blame, but I know it's my own damn fault."

I accepted his apology.

Dad's traveling companion was Annie, while I drove with Bobby, who was still nursing. We arrived dead tired, cranky, and ready for that wonderful crockpot of vegetable soup and warm Jiffy cornbread Mom knew would be just right for exhausted travelers. The next day, after emptying my truck-full of stuff into the rental storage room, we all settled into establishing a routine in their new not-quite-yet retirement house.

With Bobby strapped into the kid seat attached to the bike bumper, I spent the rest of April peddling manically through the neighborhood, singing Girl Scout camp songs as I explored tree-lined cul-de-sacs. What a joy it was to 'go a wandering', riding on flat streets with nice houses, beautiful yards, and not a mountain to be seen.

During that month I was loved back to sanity. By Mother's Day, I was calm enough to look forward. Annie played with a very happy Pop Pop, toe-touching the sky on the swing he hung from a sturdy back yard branch. We all went to Concord every Sunday. I rejoined the choir, relishing connections with those I'd known all my teen years. Mostly, however, it was a legitimate excuse every Thursday evening to go somewhere away from the constant responsibility of making sure the kids behaved. It had been many years since cartoons, crayons, and chaos consumed their lives, and this was my parents' long saved for retirement home. It was only fair that they got some semblance of peace, and I worked hard to give it to them.

One evening after practice, Mom and Daddy, looking tired and unusually serious, asked me to sit with them at the kitchen table. I noticed toys were not picked up and dirty dinner dishes still on the table.

"Kiddo, it's time to talk." Daddy's voice was quiet. "Your mother and I have something to say."

My eyes widened. "Is someone sick? Who? You should have called the church and told me."

"No one's sick and you know there isn't anyone in the office on choir night to answer the phone." She smiled. "But this is about the kids. We think it's…"

Daddy finished her sentence. "It's time for those two to have their own house."

"And you guys get back yours?" I gestured to the toys on the floor. "I understand. This is no dream retirement, what with you chasing around speedy Gonzales, her Zippy, and that little boy pill bug of a toddler. Just gotta hang in there until fall .You both know I'm trying for a teaching contract as soon as the listings go up in July. That summer school gig in '69 did give me a bit of seniority."

They exchanged looks. I noticed their tired eyes, their loving exhaustion.

"Kiddo, we have decided to help you back on your feet." Daddy stood up. "Get a job and we'll give you two thousand dollars to start off. Your mother and I feel it's time. You need to be moving forward."

"Oh, my, that's a lot of money." I had just spent six years with very little, and this amount was beyond my imagination. "Thank you so much."

"You may only spend it on rent or a mortgage," Daddy continued. "We'll help you anyway we can with old furniture and what-not, but, after this evening, we realized why God gave little ones to young people."

Mom extended her hand, taking mine across the table. "We love you all very much. We can do this together." She absently played with the wedding rings still on my finger. "You sure you want to do this? You know, the divorce."

"Yes, Mother, I do."

"Well then, don't you think you should take those things off?"

Chapter Four

Renting's ridiculous in my opinion, throwing money away, so I set my eyes on home owning. Late in May Mother asked her realtor friend to take her starry-eyed, unemployed daughter out shopping to get the feel of what kind of housing she could afford. The search was short, real short.

Gloria took me to one house, a Dutch Colonial that had seen better decades. In her best sales manner, she excused the twenty-five crumbling front steps leading from a sidewalk on the neighborhood's main artery to a non-existing front yard. "Dear, you can keep the kids safe in the backyard if you fence it off from the alley."

The Duchy had the usual, including bed rooms, bath, etc. However, this was a two-story house. She showed me a short hall ending with an obviously new set of pine steps. I climbed. *What the...* Those stairs led to a bare attic with no flooring at all, just studs with scattered chunks of insulation between.

"Dear, you can always finish off the space." Gloria was trying hard.

I walked to the front door. "No offense, but you must be out of your mind."

"My dear, now you know the challenges of unemployment. Even this house..." her voice trailed. "Well, I'm sorry."

After that little real estate misadventure, thanks to Elise Carbonare, another friend of my folks, a position with CETA was promised, starting date July first. They had all gone to high school together, and Mom played Bridge with her twice a month. She had kept 'the girls' abreast on what was going on in their house, including the realization that little ones are a whole lot more challenging than her classroom of fifth graders. Careful coffee and dessert table top conversations with Elise led to their desired conclusion. As an employment supervisor, Mrs. Carbonaro told Mom there was an opening for me.

The Comprehensive Employment and Training Act was designed to lift people out of poverty by giving paid training to work in public service. Being college educated, an assignment as job counselor was offered. This most important part of the program had me way too excited to notice my hourly pay rate was the same as the uneducated, unskilled clients I was to work with. All I knew was it was going to be in a

big office with business people in nice
clothes, not outside wearing a jumpsuit
picking up trash like I saw people working
for the department of parks. This was my
next step to independence. Mom and Dad
offered to watch the kids while I worked.
With a hug and a "No, we'll be fine", I
thanked them. Their relief was evident.

Thursday choir practice hadn't
started when, standing at my choir pew, I
announced, "Everybody, I need to ask
something." Grey heads turned my way.
"I'm looking for a house. You guys know
my story, what with living with the folks
and all." I smiled. "I get to start work soon
and we really need to be on our own."
Several in the alto section applauded. "Does
anyone know of an affordable house here in
the neighborhood?"

King of the Choir, the lead bass,
boomed, "By golly, yes ma'am, I do.
House's next door to my in-laws. The old
people are gone and the Wilkinson kids
want to sell without a realtor." He nodded to
the director, who was clearing his throat.
"We'll finish our conversation after
practice," he stage-whispered.

That night he verbally introduced me
to a two-story, three bedrooms, one bath,
years-old craftsman. The Choir King regaled
me with stories of his wife growing up next

to this house, how it held so many memories of her playing with the Wilkinson kids.

"This sounds fantastic. So, you think it would be a good place for my kids?" I especially liked the part about her playing in the old coal bin turned hideout in the basement. "Just where is this house?"

"The neighborhood used to be great. Now there's rumors that it could be changing." The Choir King hesitated. "You know where Zesty Ice Cream was on Third Street?"

"Sure. Why? I used to ride my bike there."

"Well, I hate to tell you this, but the house is on Daily Street." He grimaced. "You know what that means."

I was ecstatic. The house was inside the boundary of Wildwood School district, a neighborhood that was officially declared poverty stricken. Mom once taught there and she knew all the special services for families the school had to offer, thanks to LBJ's declaration of War On Poverty.

Daddy and I went to check it out. I loved how it looked, with white wooden siding and freshly painted green shutters framing the windows. There was a big covered porch, perfect for Mama sitting and kids playing. The front yard was small, the back yard fenced, and the street only one block long. This was not a road anyone would take to go anywhere fast.

The door had beveled glass. The sun prismed just right when we walked into the living room leading to an adjoining dining area. The walls were solid plaster and there wasn't a crack to be seen. That told me good bones. "Oh, gosh, Daddy, look at all the hardwood finishings." My gaze drifted up. "Look, look, there's an air conditioner." Smiling wistfully at him, I pointed to a small window high on the dining room far wall. "Let's see if it works. The last time I lived in air conditioning was at our old house before I went to college."

He winked and flipped the switch. It shook, growled, and then purred, blasting out sweet cold air. "Can you reach it? That button's way up there."

I giggled. "If we get this house, I'll grow taller…or at least buy a step ladder."

"Got one in the garage at home, it's all yours." He looked at the swinging door to the right of the A/C. "Let's see what's behind door number two."

We found an old-fashioned kitchen with an inviting, sunlit breakfast nook. The appliances were still there.

"Well, kiddo, will ya look at that gas stove. Wonder how old it is?" He went straight to the oven and stuck his head inside. "Pilot's lit. Don't smell fumes. That's good."

"Love cooking with gas. Brought back just the right kind of cast iron skillets from the cabin." I giggled. "Left Danny the rusty ones."

Up beautiful hardwood railed stairs there were two full bedrooms, a separate tiny nursery, and a bath. Instantly falling in love with the deep claw-footed tub, Daddy laughed as I climbed in to see if it fit. Sinking down into pretend water, I became a make-believe mermaid. The second bedroom, with no direct entrance, was accessible only through the bathroom's rear door or the room I knew would be mine. It had an alcove with a hinged cover window seat, perfect for blanket storage. I was thrilled with the house.

Daddy wasn't. "Kiddo, do you realize how close this is to Charlie's Chicken?" He made an exaggerated sniff. The house was two small bungalows and an alley away from a fast-food chicken restaurant. He didn't like the smell, I just smiled. Who could argue with the wonderful fragrance of extra crispy fried chicken?

With the assurance of that promised July job, later that week I walked into the local Winters Bank. It was just as I remembered, only smaller. The polished wood, the marble floor, the brass bars at each cashier station had not changed. Everyone who ever banked there wanted to catch a glimpse of the family's famous relative, Jonathan. Not many did, but there was always that chance.

"Ma'am?" My voice was hesitant as I stood before a middle-aged, bee-hived hair sprayed to 1960's perfection caged lady.

The teller looked up. "Yes?"

"I'm going to need a mortgage." I smiled. "Soon."

She smiled back. "Really, how soon?"

"As soon as work starts July first."

She stopped smiling. "What is your name? Do you have an account here? Who is your husband? Can't get a loan without him, you know." She opened a wooden box sitting before her. It looked like one of those recipe card holders given as wedding shower gifts.

"I used to when I was a teenager," I blurted. "Then I was Susan Taylor. Still am. Kept my name. I want you to know I'm really good with money, saving all my babysitting pay back then. It sure helped with college, and I'm proud to say that I graduated in three years. Now I'm married," making a face, added, "but not for long."

She rifled through the cards under T. "Parents lived at 428 Moonshadow? I see they moved."

"Uh huh. They gave me two thousand dollars for a down payment on the house I found for me and my children. Also, I'll need a check book once I start work. You know, to make payments with."

The teller pursed her lips. "Let me get the mortgage manager. Please wait." She put a cardboard CLOSED sign at the opening of her cage and disappeared for what seemed way too long.

A white haired, pinstriped man walked up beside me. "Suzie? Don't tell me it's my little Suzie Q." His broad smile looked so familiar. "It's Mr. Ressler, your old Sunday school teacher. My goodness, you look like your daddy. You know, we used to bowl together in the church league before he hurt his knee. "

Mr. Ressler was my favorite at Evening Vacation Bible School. He knew all the songs, and when us kids would sing *'Joy, joy, joy, joy'*, he would sing *'Down in my heart'* in a really deep voice. The girls would sing high and squeaky *'Down in my heart'* to answer his bass. We always ended up in a fit of giggles.

"Hi, how are you?" I grinned. "Do you bank here, too?"

The lady, back in her cage, cleared her throat. "It looks like you don't need an introduction to our mortgage manager." She flipped her sign to OPEN.

"Come into my office, and catch me up on where you have been all these years. I was just told you zipped your way through college, are married but not for long, there are children, and that you haven't started working yet. Also, you found a house you want to buy, your folks gave you the down payment, and that you are good with money. Is that everything in a nut shell? Anything else I need to know?"

"No sir. Everything seems covered." I paused. "There's only one thing."

Mr. Ressler tilted his head. "What would that be?"

"It's on Daily Street, in the Wildwood School district. You know what that means."

His eyes crinkled. "You mean to tell me that you have found a house that your daddy approves of down the street from my favorite chicken joint? Well, whataya know." He grinned. "Oh, you mean you're worried about the neighborhood?"

I nodded.

"Well, from a financial point, you made a good choice. That poverty war we're supposedly fighting is allowing for lower mortgage interest rates in certain areas." He looked at the back of his office door. "Let's see if Daily Street is on this map."

It was. Several phone calls later, all was settled. The Wilkinson kids said we could move in with a rent-to-own private contract when my new life started in the summer. I would send them Mr. Ressler's suggested monthly mortgage payments, including the lower interest. In return they would apply principal payments to the selling price, keeping the extra as rent. This coming January I would be a legal state resident, and could finalize the dissolution. Then I'd apply for a mortgage using Mom and Dad's down payment without any strings attached.

All was settled. We were to move in the last week of June. Once again Daddy's pickup was put to use. I had my Granddad's four-poster, the sofa and chair set, my beloved baby rocker, piano...and Daddy's high chair. We emptied the rental storage unit. My parents, relatives, and even the original home owner' kids scrabbled together enough furniture to make the new place a home. They even found a bed and crib for the kids. I was overwhelmed with gratitude...and used pots and pans.

Chapter Five

Wildwood School offered free half day Head Start, another weapon in the War. Highly paid poverty specialists around the country realized that children learn young. Geez, I could have told them that and saved the government a pile of money.

Before she was transferred to Patterson, Mom taught fifth grade for several years at Wildwood, loving the diversity of cultures, including first and second generation Appalachian migrants making good money at General Motors. These families were open with their love and homemade biscuits. Wildwood was the only naturally integrated school in this part of a severely divided city. Ruby Avenue, known for the New Orleans style shotgun houses, was black long before the politicians got involved. Therefore, Mom's classrooms were always mixed.

She loved to tell her spelling test story around the card table.

Mom---Spell 'help'.

Student #1---Huh?

Mom---'Help', spell 'help'.

Student #2 to Student #1---She means 'hep', but she don't talk so good.

Then she'd smile, remembering her own carefully removed Southern accent and her grandmother's voice.

Stately old Victorians, divided into apartments, held lots of children. Mom taught three of Ruth Williams' many kids and knew 'Mammaw' was the one sitter all the neighborhood mothers trusted. Her house was whole, and as each of her many children left for adult lives, Ruth took in 'keepers'. As a favor to mom, she agreed to watch my kids full time, and when school started in September, Annie could walk three blocks to the school's side entrance where little ones got their head start. We were finally on our own.

That magical day in July, children happily swallowed up by the Williams family, I went to work at the unemployment office, proudly wearing a new business pants suit, learning how to place the needy in government sponsored jobs. A week later reality hit when I got my first check. I was one of the needy. Making even less than I ever imagined, there was not one cent extra once the house, babysitter, and utilities were paid.

My supervisor, Mrs. Carbonaro, found me crying at my desk. "What's going on? What happened?"

Showing her the check, I sobbed. "I, I can't buy food, I can't make it work. Oh, my lord, I can't feed the kids." Three months of fear, anxiety, and heart-broken loss poured out of me, right there in front of my new boss.

She stood, waiting for the tears to subside before pointing at the check. "It's for your first week, not the whole pay period." She tapped the work dates on the stub. "Double the amount. This will all work out." She smiled. "Blow your nose."

I grabbed a tissue, wiped my eyes, blew, and looked up at her. "How? Right now I can't even buy bread and milk."

"See your check? See the word CETA on it?" She tapped the stub again. "This program is for working people of poverty, and honey, you're not only poor, you're plain po'." She pulled one of the folded brochures in the plastic case on my desk. "You qualify for food stamps."

"Oh, no, not again," I moaned.

She ignored me. "Take your stub and all your bills, including what you pay the sitter to the Department of Social Services. Do you get child support?"

"No. We're not legal yet," I made a face, "and he refuses to pay for anything. The man has not worked in a year, but says he will support his children when I come to my senses and move back." I shrugged. "Did come to my senses. I'm here."

"That's what your mom said at cards. I'm not supposed to tell, but the Bridge girls know all about you. She's really glad you came home." Elise touched her index finger to her lips. "Your mom is so proud of how independent you are. However, we can't talk anymore about personal stuff here in the office."

I nodded. "Thanks for telling me. I'm glad Mom feels that way."

Mrs. Carbonaro tilted her head to the left. "You know DSS is next door in the old Red Feather Building. Tomorrow, when I see you at your desk, go take care of business on the clock." She nodded, tapping her lips again. "Just keep hush about it."

"Yes, ma'am, thank you, but, but what about until I get the stamps? What can I do?"

"Look on the back of the brochure. Your job is to help people. Consider this part of your training."

She left me blowing my nose. Sure enough, there in the three-column list of locations, open every evening five to seven, was a free neighborhood pantry in the Wildwood School basement. I went there straight from work and had to show them my paystub. Food banks check to see if you're poor, even if you are wearing a fancy pants suit. They gave me a cardboard box of basic staples, including flour, sugar, one dozen eggs, and macaroni.

I never told my parents. That night I made supper using elbows and some thickened powdered milk with yellow food coloring to fake the cheese, stirring in what I had left of a mostly gone block of Velveeta. Annie loved her 'macky cheese', Bobby, now almost a year old, picked up each elbow off his highchair tray, delighting in feeding himself. I ate what was left straight from the pan. We survived.

Chapter Six

God bless the War On Poverty. The Elementary and Secondary Education Act poured millions of dollars into qualified schools. October brought the call to fill a one-year ESEA Reading Tutor contract at Mill Run Primary, hiring me as a full-time substitute with benefits. The pay was about the same as at the CETA office. It still kept me on food stamps and little Miss Head Start eating free school lunches. However, I was finally teaching again, getting a bit of seniority for that hoped for regular contract next year.

Our wonderful symbol of independence with its big front porch, sturdy walls and fenced yard had an unused formal dining room. I converted it to a playroom for the kids, furnished with a castoff dining captain's chair, and a small table with a new thirteen inch TV. Also, there was a Castro Convertible loveseat we used as a couch. This was the room with that miraculously running old rusty air conditioner requiring my daddy's step stool. Cool air, ahh, what joy, what luxury.

The dining/playroom also had a double window alcove just like my bedroom with a built-in bench hiding the radiator vents. I was way too busy for cushion sewing, so it quickly became a clutter catcher, covered with books, toys and general kid mess. Vicky Walters, teacher in the next classroom down the hall, gave me a giant, three-foot-wide hand-me-down philodendron. She'd named the thing Grindle because she thought it looked like something from a fairy tale forest. I didn't argue that one. The thing had thrived in the humidity of twenty four little ones, sweating away their ABCs. The plant loved the sun. Vicky'd found out she was being moved to a basement interior room. Silly me told her I had a sunny spot at home. Next thing ya know, it was in the center of the playroom bench, taking up most of the window.

Someone had attached a metal plant hanger between the windows; probably Mrs. Wilkinson sometime in the '60's when avocado green or harvest gold macramé covered each and every flower pot in the whole wide world. The hook was about three and a half feet above the window seat. I never hung any living thing from it, just miscellaneous orphan socks found in the bottom of the basket as I sorted laundry in front of my first ever color TV. This room, next to the kitchen, usually considered the heart of every home, became the main artery that kept our house alive. This was our real living room.

***

Bobby moaned in his sleep. I heard nothing. He cried out in his wakening. I heard nothing. Then he screamed. I ran, nightgown flying, to find him standing in his crib, eyes wide, unseeing. Flipping on the overhead light, I screamed too. That brought Annie and, of course, Zippy.

"Mommy, Mommy, look at him, look at his face. It's fat." She worked her way between me and the crib, reaching through the bars for her brother's legs. "Mommy, something's really wrong. He's all red."

My little boy's face was unrecognizable, swollen to the size of a cantaloupe. In front of his right ear was a lump, resembling a purple tangerine. If it weren't so close to Halloween, I wouldn't have realized that Bobby looked just like a Hob Goblin. I also realized that we had to go to Children's Hospital. Now.

Getting us ready seemed to take forever. Bobby was still in diapers and happened to be especially messy. Annie proudly dressed herself and I didn't notice until much later that her shirt was inside out and shoes wrong footed. Me, well, let's just say that I was lucky that yesterday's school outfit was crumpled on the floor by my bed and hadn't yet found the dirty clothes basket. Fresh undies, yes, bra, got one hook done. We were on our way. It was around three in the morning. The streets offered no traffic. I sped.

Bobby in arms, Annie and Zippy in hand, we ran through the Emergency Room's automatic doors. The triage nurse was sitting at her desk, waiting for disasters. It was evident by her face that we didn't qualify.

Looking at me, she said, "Do you have insurance?" I nodded. "What happened?" She waited.

"I don't know what happened." I started to cry. "I don't know. He woke up screaming. I just don't know."

"Did he fall out of bed?" The nurse was writing on a clip board.

"Oh, no," Annie piped up. "He was in his bed, wasn't he, Mommy."

The nurse stood. "Is he your little brother?"

"Uh huh," her bottom lip trembling, "Can you fix him? He's my friend. I love him." She held up her monkey. "So does Zippy. He's really scared."

The nurse pulled a couple of yellow striped Band-Aids from her pocket. "Do you think yellow will help?" She started herding us down the hall.

Annie's eyes lit up. "Yes! Curious George's best friend is the man in the yellow hat. Zippy likes yellow, too."

"Do you want me to help Zippy stop being scared? Band-Aids fix everything. Would you like a yellow one, too?" The nurse looked for my nod of approval. "You'd be matching."

"Uh huh, please. On our heads like a yellow hat." Annie pulled back her hair, pointing to her forehead. "Right there."

The nurse held out her arms for Bobby, now all interested in his surroundings, crying long stopped. "We have a room ready for his checkup." She handed over the Band-Aids. "If you don't mind, could you fix up Sissy and Zippy? We're going to start an IV. Probably better those two don't watch." I nodded. The nurse smiled. "He will get something to help him rest while we find out what's going on. Oh, by the way," she looked at Annie, "good to see she's been read to. I can tell."

Sitting beside that emergency room crib, I softly sang to the very scared big sister curled up, dozing in my lap. I watched the now sleeping little brother being expertly cared for. Several hours and many tests later we were sent home with an appointment for a CT scan later that day.

I took Annie to Mammaw Williams' house as soon as I thought it was acceptable. When she saw Bobby and I told her why, she got over her two hour early drop off grumpies. "Go find breakfast, child, and for goodness sake, turn your shirt right side around. Don't forget to feed your monkey; there's bananas in the kitchen."

I got a Mammaw hug after Annie headed off. "I know what a CT scan means. I will pray."

I hugged her back. "Thank you. Can Annie stay past pick up time? It's scheduled for two. I don't know how long…"

"Good Lord, of course. Don't you worry about a thing." She smiled. "I've learned to just give that girl a jar of Jif and a loaf of bread. She and that monkey can survive in a deserted island." Kissing Bobby on the other side of his purple cheek, she admonished me to 'get that boy something to eat' and to 'make sure he doesn't miss his nap before you go back to the hospital'.

He refused to eat. After I got him rocked to sleep, I called school. There were no substitutes for tutors and no pay for me missing a day. The secretary just asked my name.

At noon, two hours before the appointment, I took us to the one place all distressed daughters go. In the hallway outside my mother's classroom, handing over my misshapen son to his grandmother, I cried. We both cried. This new form of diagnosis was used for one thing only, tumors. They were checking my child for cancer.

The test was a blur. Results came swiftly. The doctors were reassuring. I laughed. My goblin headed baby had an impacted first molar. The treatment...time worn. Hold warm washrags to his cheek, and give him an old piece of leather to chew on.

Mother offered the best advice of all. "Your grandmother says to pour a shot of bourbon. Dip your finger and rub his sore gums, then you drink the whiskey. Repeat as needed."

I followed her advice to a T. The tooth erupted and I found out that I liked the taste of Jim Beam. All was well.

From that day forward until they both went to college, I slept in a fully hooked bra, just in case.

Chapter Seven

"Mommy, Mommy, look what we did in school today."

"Good grief, child. We just got home. Let me get the house unlocked."

Annie was skipping and hopping in circles all the way from the car to the porch, her end of day frazzled pigtails flying. Standing Bobby down on the sidewalk, I jingled out my keyring, looking for the biggest one. "Hang loose, goose, gotta find the right key." Bobby made a quick turn toward the street. Dropping the ring, diaper bag, and briefcase full of papers to grade, I raced to the curb, grabbing that boy with more force than needed, causing him to holler. Spinning him to face the steps, I swatted his well-cushioned behind.

Bobby's protests didn't seem to dampen Annie's school enthusiasm. "Mommy, Mommy, we made a turkey out of our hand. All we had to do was open our fingers and draw." Her circle dance halted square in front of me, hair-covered eyes giving me the once over. "Um, Mommy, you dropped your stuff." She snatched up the ring. "I know the right key. Can I unlock the front door?" Noticing her brother's tears, she added, "I'll let him turn the knob."

"Remind me to fix your tails."

She reached up and expertly pulled out her blue elastics, shaking her head like a lion,freed mane flying. "OK, but only if you use the red bands and not pull them too tight. You make my eyes bug out."

"I do not."

"Uh huh."

In the time I got my work clothes changed, Annie had Bobby in his highchair, tracing his hand, making more turkeys. I stood quietly, peeking through the crack of the ajar kitchen door, watching my four year old running her own classroom. She traced and he scribbled feathers all over the page. She raggedly cut out each hand turkey with some preschool scissors I snagged from the Kindergarten supply closet. My mom would have a fit if she knew I was letting her only granddaughter cut paper. Scissors were scary, but I knew this was not my project.

"Mommy, could you come here a minute? We've got something to show you."

Her voice wasn't urgent. Guess there was no blade injury. "Sure Punkin' what is it?" I swung open the door. The floor was practically covered with hand print turkeys. I looked at them both, grinned, pretended to pull the string, and quoted their Fischer Price Farmer See and Say. "What does the turkey say?"

"Gobble, gobble, gobble," they yelled in unison.

Annie's hair never got done that day, too many turkeys running around.

Thanksgiving was wonderful and sad all at the same time. My grandmother's table overflowed with the holiday foods my mother'd grown up with, all served since, well, forever. However, for the last six years, I'd feasted with my husband's family and learned to love their special foods. My mother-in-law introduced me to scalloped oysters, creamed pearl onions, and a delightful concoction of ground cranberries, oranges, and English walnut halves, just to name a few of what I considered exotic dishes That slice of canned jellied glop in front of me did not hold a candle to what she called her 'grind up'.

Sitting with my children and the other small ones at the kiddy table, listening to 'Come Lord Jesus' prayed in German, I mourned what could have been. No one knew how much my other mother was missed. She'd been raised in New York City and had a sophisticated palate. She brought this with her into her marriage. Pleasing her husband with fine cooking was expected and I appreciated her skills.

The kiddy seating assignment was not my idea. My grandmother explained to me that there was an even number of chairs around the dining table, and because I was a 'singleton', and since I was used to kids anyway, she thought it perfect that I sit in a chair built for five-year olds. I knew this was her way of saying that, without a husband, I didn't fit in the family anymore.

Bobby ate 'gobble gobble and mashies'. Annie watched her two girl cousins and pretended to be a picky eater, refusing to taste anything green. I threatened no pumpkin pie for picky Patty and all of a sudden, her plate was clean. I didn't care what the cousins did. Their married mommas were busy having grown up conversations, a commodity I craved. If they wanted their girls to earn dessert, they can just get themselves over to the little chairs. That didn't happen.

The cousins were chattering away about what their Mommies and Daddies did. Annie looked to me, all puzzled. "You're a teacher. What does Daddy do? Go on big car trips?"

I was shocked. In all these months, she hadn't even mentioned him. Not once. I thought she'd forgotten that trip to

Colorado, everything about our past life. I was wrong.

"Um, Punkin', I don't know what Daddy does. What do you remember?" *I was on thin ice, not wanting anyone around to hear this exchange, lest my tone get interpreted as whiny. This exile to the kiddy table was rough enough; I didn't need my aunt with her 'perfect' family of daughters expressing her dismay for my so-called failure.*

"I remember we went on a big trip with Daddy and ate turkey when we got there." Her eyes were far off. "I think we had cousins there, too."

"Yes, there were cousins. Anything else?"

"I remember that Daddy and the cousins' daddy made firecrackers." She smiled. "That's what he does, fires firecrackers." She turned back to the cousins at hand. "My daddy drives a car and makes noise. That's all I know." The cousins seemed impressed.

Chapter Eight

The first Sunday of Advent arrived right on schedule. I was thrilled to see the church at Thursday's choir practice. Fresh pine garlands, draped in swags and wreaths throughout, filled the sanctuary. The fragrance was wonderful. Just for fun we started the Christmas rehearsal with 'Deck the Halls'.

After practice, and putting away my music folder with the others, I quietly walked the perimeter of the room. Everything smelled so clean. There was a moment of rest in my soul. Stopping at the communion table, I admired the candles and empty manger, knowing that this Sunday the hand carved olive wood animals from Bethlehem would be in place, waiting for human visitors traveling on their journey.

I always left the kids down in the church basement nursery to play during practice, and I wasn't quite ready to get back into Mommy mode. Turning the corner to go into the narthex, I discovered a pile of pine scraps. They weren't roped together, or formed into a wreath, or tied up as a garland.

They were definitely discards. With no one close to stop me, I gathered as much as I could and headed down the hall to the parking lot.

The choir director came up beside me. "Need a hand? I can get you more if you want."

"Would you, Clarence? I'm always scratching around for free things." I looked up at him. "These are left overs, right? Kinda like gleaning?"

"He shrugged. "I guess so. The pile's been there since Tuesday. Are you planning to do anything with this stuff? My Martha uses really thin wire and makes door decorations. Maybe you could, too." He loaded his arms and followed to my car, talking all the way. "Yep, Marty buys wire from McCrory's down in Airway Shopping Center. I guess it's in the sewing and crafts section. She puts the pine boughs on a metal form and wraps the stems with wire." He smiled. "Add a big bow and there ya go. We have one on our front door right now."

"Is it hard to do?" I juggled my load to open the car trunk. "If there's one thing I'm not, is artsy-crafty."

"She says her hands remind her of pine trees for days, what with the sap sticking." He piled his load on top of mine. "You think you can close that thing? Your car's going to be ready for Christmas now. And to think people hang cardboard trees from their rearview mirror to get what you've got naturally."

"Thank you for helping with the branches."

He slammed the lid and turned to me, eyes darkening.

"Sue." His voice was low, soft, and ominous, all at the same time. "Sue, I've been talked to by the powers-that-be about your kids." He shook his head. "There's a problem."

I froze. "What problem?" I knew they were behaving, playing in the nursery. One of them would've come to find me if they weren't. "They're good kids."

The choir director stared over my head. "I'm supposed to tell you that you can't leave them in the basement." Sighing, he rushed on. "The deacons heard from… well, it was reported by a certain choir member that you are a negligent mother, leaving 'em unsupervised during practice. Head Deacon Huffman came to me, asked if it was true, and said that unattended children in the church might be an insurance liability."

"I doubt that," steel slipping into my voice, "but, what with the cost of babysitting, the only way I can afford to attend choir practice is to bring my children with me. AND, since one of my fellow choir members, and I can guess that it's Beatrice, seems to have no understanding for my situation, I quit."

"But…" Clarence finally looked at me.

The steely tones were solid iron. "You can rest assured that there will be no more problems. This negligent mother will gather up your possible liabilities and go home."

"But…"

"You don't get it, do you? A sitter's five dollars an hour, money I don't have. Choir practice is my only outlet all week." Turning to the church door, I threw over my shoulder, "Tell that to your puppet master Deacon Big Shot, and, and Her Royal Hind End, Mrs. Queen Bee."

His "But…" bounced off the door slammed behind me. I took my kids and the purloined pine branches home, calling Mom as soon as the kids were in bed. Crying, I told her what happened and who I thought had complained. We agreed.

"That old witch with a B," she said. "You know, she's the reason I quit the Concord Deaconesses years ago. You'd think she was born wearing a crown, the way she acts."

"Yeah," I sniffled. "She's got horns holding up that crown."

"Now, now..." I could practically see Mom shaking her head on the other end of the line. "Are you leaving the church, too? Daddy and I sure would miss our Sundays all together."

"No, just quitting choir. That one hour of church is one hour of peace. I wouldn't give that up." I looked away from the phone. "Oh, by the way, I have a bunch of pine branches here in the playroom. Got 'em from the cast-off pile after the sanctuary was decorated. Don't know what I'll do with them, but they sure smell good."

"Pine branches?" Her voice rose. "Get them out side before they start seeping. They're gonna leave goo on your carpet, and that stuff is as sticky as chewing gum."

"Really? Now? They smell so good."

"Now." My mother was bossy, but this night I needed that. "Put them out in the cold. The house heat will get the sap running. Do it now."

"Yes, ma'am."

Chapter Nine

The living room had a beautiful cherry mantel over a gas fireplace. The Wilkinson family obviously hung Christmas stockings because cup hooks were attached underneath. It was the type of fireplace with ceramic gridding in front, not fake logs. I was scared of it, remembering those open flames my Great Aunt Emma used to heat her parlor. I never lit ours. I didn't mention anything about mantels, stockings, or the such to the kids. I couldn't afford a tree and had very little money for presents. I was banking on the gifts from their father. Besides, no Santa in his right mind would come down that chimney and land on a fake fireplace, flames or not.

I didn't foresee the enthusiasm of Wildwood School's Head Start's teacher. Just like those Thanksgiving turkeys, all of sudden Annie was deep into free-handing Christmas trees. This time, tracing her fingers closed and coloring different colored balls where the fingernails should be, she was making a forest. This artistry started the questions, the topic of which I was so carefully avoiding, questions of a tree in our house.

"Mommy, Mommy, Mommy, come here." The kitchen floor was once again covered, this time with sorta green-colored Christmas trees decorated with sorta fingernail-shaped red balls. "I made the trees; Bobby colored the balls." She ran to his highchair and held up the preschool crayon. "I gave him red 'cause that's the only one we had in the box that was fat enough for him to hold without breaking." She smiled. "Can we hook all of them together and make decorations? Mrs. Cunningham stapled everybody's trees together in a chain. We could do that for our tree."

There it was, "our tree". *Damn.* A live tree was so beyond my budget, and those new plastic trees, even more so. How was I going to tell my bright beautiful child that there would be no tree for Santa, no place to put presents? Picking up the scattered hand tracings, I didn't say a word.

Annie noticed, her lower lip starting to pout. "Mommy, what's the matter? Don't you like them? Aren't they pretty enough? Are they too scribbly?"

"No, sweetheart, no." *Think fast.* "It's just the opposite."

"What does opposite mean?" She held up one of her masterpieces. "I thought 'possoms hung by their tails and didn't sit." She studied her work, turned it up side down, and held it out to me. "It doesn't even look like a 'possom sittin'."

"Oh, you silly bump." I smooched her offering and then her head. "Opposite means the other way. You know, like you are opposite from Bobby, girl to boy." I slid back Bobby's highchair tray and he scooted out, bee-lining for one of the more spotted trees.

"I make, I make." Off he ran to the playroom. Annie and I followed.

"So, you like them?" She held two paper trees side by side. "Can we make a chain decoration like at school?"

"Yes, but not for a Christmas tree, we need to decorate um, uh..." My eyes fell on the window seat. "We need to decorate Grindle." I stuck one of the paper trees in between the branches of that giant monstrosity. "Yep, Grindle needs a chain of decorations." I grabbed the stapler from my briefcase. "Let's make a chain for Grindle. She's part of our family, too."

I got a four year old eye roll. "Mommy, just to let you know, Griddle's a plant, not a people."

"Zippy's part of our family, he's not a people, either." I was grasping at straws.

"That's different. Zippy's mine."

"Well, Grindle's ours, so there." *Please, child, just let it go.* Annie looked at me, waiting. "She's big enough to be an animal," I continued. "What's your favorite pretend dog? You know, the one in the story we read at bedtime?" *I was trying the impossible task of redirecting her. Hah!*

"You mean Clifford? He's a big red dog."

"Yes. We can call Grindle our pet, an imaginary dog without the bark."

Annie started laughing. "Mommy, I get it. Grindle's not a tree 'cause she's got stems and doesn't have bark. So, she can be our Christmas Dog Bush." She snatched up my stapler. "I can do it."

"No baby, your fingers are just the right size for getting in the wrong places." I took back the tool. "You two gather all the trees you made and let's decorate our Christmas dog."

Bobby's eyes went wide. "Doggy? Woof Woof? For me?"

"No woof woof," his sister answered, "Christmas Dog Bush."

"Doggy, doggy, doggy!"

"Stop it, you two. Enough is enough." I picked up my boy, hushed him, and sat him on the love seat. "Annie and I are going to decorate Grindle. You watch."

I stapled, Annie draped, Bobby barked. Grindle the Christmas Dog Bush didn't say a word.

That night my children's world came tumbling down, and thank goodness, they never knew. My soon-to-be ex called late, after the long-distance charges changed, to drop his bomb. I picked up the phone on first ring, thinking the worst.

"Who died?" I blurted.

"Hello to you, too." I knew the voice instantly. The sharp-edged, beer blurred tone brought back those last few days together.

"Uh, hi." I swallowed. "Sorry for the 'died' part. It's just that no one calls me late on a school night. What do you want?"

He laughed. "I'm just callin' to tell you that I'm not sendin' anything to the kids for Christmas. I told Mom and Dad not to, either."

I was dumbfounded, no words to say.

"Ya wanna know why?"

"Yes."

"'Cause all ya have ta do is come back to me."

"But we agreed…"

"The kids can open all their presents here." He chuckled again. "Ya see, it's that easy."

I took a deep breath, mustering my calmest voice, and said, "Go to hell." I slammed down the phone as my heart crashed closed, knowing I was utterly and completely alone.

That night I dreamed of giant decorated trees marching in rows, throwing boxes of glass ornaments here and there. Each decoration exploded and made tiny little marching trees. This forest of marching and exploding multiplied until all I saw was the sway of the trees and the glitter of the glass bombs. Suddenly, like nuclear fallout, I was covered in blood in a dust field of flying ornament shards.

I woke up sweat-drenched, shaking, and gasping for air that would not come.

Chapter Ten

The start of school vacation, always scheduled the week before Christmas, lasting 'til the Monday after New Year's. Unlike our home, my classroom was festooned to the hilt. Using construction paper from the supply closet, I did there what I couldn't do at our house. Swiping those glorious sheets of crafting goodness never once occurred to me.

What did occur was to repeat what happened my eighth-grade year. The neighborhood school had a welcoming front vestibule, and every Christmas the most gloriously long soft needles covered with students' best offerings greeted all visitors. When I was in the seventh grade, I saw the custodian put that beautiful tree out back in the trash bin. I promised myself that next year, when I would be older and stronger, I would save the tree from the rubbish and drag it home. And I did.

My parents' house was exactly one mile from the grade school. Mom and Dad always got a short prickly needled tree. Even though I hated the feel of the family

Christmas tree, I had no right to criticize their choice, so I dragged that sweet soft pine home for a holiday surprise, hoping they couldn't resist. They were not pleased. However, after begging my heart out, they did set it up in the basement rec room, leaving their prickly pear by the living room fireplace.

Now, as a teacher, I just knew that the tree in this school's hallway could be rescued like the other one. There was only one problem. Me, the one year ESEA contracted reading tutor didn't need to be seen rummaging through the trash. I figured it wouldn't bode well for me getting a new contract for next year.

Mrs. Woodly, secretary and keeper of all things Principal related, sat clicking at her precious Selectric typewriter. Eventually looking up from her beautifully manicured red nails, she finally noticed me on the other side of the front counter. It was well known that no teacher, new or seasoned, could step through the swinging gate that protected her and the inner sanctum called the Principal's Office, and her boss, Mrs. Adkins.

"Oh, it's you, the new girl. Got a bad kid to leave off?" She looked back at her keyboard and started typing away.

"Um, no." Clearing my throat to get her attention again, I went right to the point.

"Do you think it would be possible for me to ask Mrs. Adkins if I could take home the hallway Christmas tree the last day before break? I'd hate to see it thrown away."

"You are new, aren't you?" *Click clickity.* "Everyone knows that *I* decorate the hall tree and *I* take it home." *Clickity click click.* Her voice rose. "That tree is mine; do you understand me?" *Clack clack clack.*

I turned, leaving the office before she could see tears welling, my last chance dashed by a red clawed dragon roaring behind her castle wall.

***

One thing good about Christmas was the annual reruns of all holiday cartoons. Rudolph, Frosty, Little Drummer Boy, you name it; they were TV's standard fare. Before I had kids, I righteously vowed to never use the tube as a baby sitter. What a shallow promise that was. Making a list of every show on my three available channels, I put the kids in their jammies and plopped them in front of every one of them. The shows bought me much desired paper grading time.

"Mommy, Mommy, come look. Charlie Brown has the silliest Christmas tree."

I pretended not to hear. "Mommy, Mommy, Momeee, ya gotta see." Annie bounced into the kitchen and grabbed my arm. "Come on, Mommy, come on. Watch with us."

"Okay, in a minute, only three more tests to go." I looked up from the table into her shining eyes, and laid down my red pen. *Phooey on phonics*.

After 'A Charlie Brown Christmas' and a bazillion toy commercials, Disney's 'Fantasia' came on. I loved this movie and, having watched it since my own childhood, had most scenes memorized. All was fun until 'Sorcerer's Apprentice'. The part where the spells get out of hand had both kids burrowed in my sides, too frightened to watch. I stared at the screen, loving the music and Mickey's magic. When the really terrifying 'Night on Bald Mountain' came on, I quickly declared bedtime, snapping off the set. Scooping up Bobby, we pretended to be dancing elephants all the way up the steps. Annie flapped her pig tails like giant ears and swayed her bottom, using her hand behind her like a swishing tail. Kissing them good night, I giggled at the thought of boozy pink elephants instead of sugar plums dancing in their heads.

That night something woke me. "Oh," I said out loud, sitting straight up in bed, startled out of my dream. It was way past midnight and the house was silent. Not taking time to put on slippers and robe, I checked my sleeping kids. All was well. Smiling, I tucked Zippy back in her mommy's arm. *No loose monkeys swinging around this bedroom tonight.* Cupping a cold drink of water from the bathroom sink, I sat at the top of the steps and cried thankful tears. Now I knew why I had that ornament shattering dream. Mister Mickey Mouse and Concord Presbyterian Church were going to save our Christmas.

Chapter Eleven

This year's vacation came late on the calendar, leaving little preparation time. I decided to spin the 'no tree for Santa' story into a 'maybe a tree for Santa'. I handled the problem by telling the true tale of my dad's childhood tradition. I gathered my sweeties to each side of me on the love seat with a promise of a 'once uppa time' as Annie called my many made up bedtime stories.

I began. "Pop Pop's Christmas was very special when he was little."

Annie elbowed me. "Mommy, you forgot."

"Forgot what? I just started." This was a game we played every story time.

She looked at her brother. "Ready?" He grinned. "One, two, three. Once uppa time," they chimed, Bobby getting the 'time' out nice and clear.

"Okay, okay, here we go. One upon a time, Pop Pop's Christmas was very special when he was little."

She shook her head. "You already said that."

"Missy," I threatened. She hushed. "Anyway, his mommy and daddy, called Gee-Gee Mom Mom and Gee-Gee Pop Pop, never had a tree until Christmas Eve, and it only came after the kids went to bed."

"Why? That sounds mean. They didn't get to look at it early." Bobby echoed her 'mean'.

"Well, back in the olden days, Santa brought the tree, decorations and all, down the chimney when he came to fill the stockings. The Gee Gees had a giant fireplace."

Annie's bottom slid off the couch, ran to the living room, and stood, hands on hips. She studied our ceramic fireplace. Pirouetting, she made an exaggerated pout and dramatically plopped back in her story listening spot. "Can't happen here," she sighed. "No room."

"Huh?" Bobby was becoming a fairly good listener...for an eighteen month old toddler. "No room for Caw Caus? I want Caw Caus. I want Caw Caus tree."

"You two just stop and listen to the story. You know the rules. One---sit still, two---listen close, three---?" I waited.

"Tell it back to Mommy."

Hugging them both, I responded, "Yes ma'am. You guys tell me the story back." I kissed both heads and continued.

"Our Pop Pop was just a little boy when they had a really bad snow storm. By Christmas Eve there was so much snow falling that boots were not high enough. No one could go in or out."

"Not even to make a snowman? I made a snowman with Pop Pop last year. We named him Frosty." My Wiggle Worm scooted off her spot and began pantomiming rolling a snowman head. Mid-roll she saw me holding up a finger. "Uh oh, rule one." She landed back into her seat.

"To continue…" my tone said more than words could. "Pop Pop and his sister, Auntie Marie, knew Santa couldn't come. The storm was really, really bad." I shook my head. "Pop Pop told me they fell asleep crying." Miss Wiggles opened her mouth, saw my glare and decided against saying anything.

"Pop Pop cry?" Bobby hadn't gotten the 'hush up' message. "Poor sad Pop Pop."

"Anyway, Pop Pop and Auntie Marie finally fell asleep. The next morning, they didn't want to get up, what with no tree, no Santa, just snowstorm. Finally, Great Grand Mom Mom came upstairs into their room, fussing that breakfast was getting cold and they'd better go into the kitchen right now if they knew what was good for them." I took an extra deep breath. "When they got down, they saw the biggest, prettiest, most wonderful Christmas tree. Pop Pop said the bright lights made him blink. And their stockings were filled, too. His mommy told them to look outside. He said the snow was up to the front porch, all smooth and sparkly, and there weren't even dog tracks in it." I stopped talking, waiting for the story telling game to continue.

Annie played. "And then?"

"And then nothing. That's when Pop Pop knew that Santa was as magical as they said. Nobody could have brought a giant tree down a chimney or in a front door without out messing up the snow. They had a very merry Christmas. The end."

"All right, all right, I'll tell it back." Annie smiled. "Rudolph, with your nose so bright, won't you guide my sleigh tonight? The end."

"Huh?" That girl was just plain silly.

"Knows who seepin', knows who wake. Caw Caus come to town. De end." Bobby's singing surprised me. Guess he had been listening to the cartoons. "Caw Caus down our cimmey?"

"I don't think so." Annie stood before us, her four-year old arms folded all serious like, face all squinched. "Mommy, tell him."

"Tell him what?" *I knew what was coming next. This little girl must have known we had no money, no tree, no presents, and that her father was a royal jerk.* "Tell him what?"

Taking her brother by the hand, she walked solemnly to the living room and turned him, facing our filled hearth. "Bobby, I hate to tell you this, but Santa is way too fat to come down that chimney and bring a tree and presents, too." She pointed at the ceramic grid, shaking her head. "That thing's in the way. It would poke his behind. We just gotta leave the front door unlocked."

Whew, dodged that bullet. Now on to my dreamed tree plan. "I think you're right. Let's leave the door unlocked." Gently guiding them away from the hearth to the door, I opened it. "Annie, spread your arms and check the size. That will tell us how big a tree we will get."

Annie did the "so big' arm spread and determined that Santa could put his present pack on the porch, bring in the tree, and then go back for the gifts. Thank goodness her arm spread was little girl size.

"Me do. Me do." Bobby did his baby sized measure. *Ah, even better.* "Caw Caus comin' ta town."

"Yes. Santa will come and put something in your stockings just like at Pop Pop's when he was a boy."

Annie's face fell. "No unwraps? We've been good."

I smiled. "Oh, I forgot to tell you, Mom Mom told me that she wrote a letter to Santa and asked him to leave all your presents there. You know they have a real fireplace, not a pretend one like ours."

Annie squinched her mouth, tilted her head, thought a bit and declared that it just might work. "So, do we still leave him cookies and milk, or does Mom Mom do it?"

"We do it. Mom Mom does it, too."

She spun around and ran toward the kitchen. "That's gonna be one fat Santa," she threw over her shoulder.

I heard the fridge door open. "Child, what are you getting into now?"

"We gotta go to the store," she hollered. "No carrots for Rudolph."

"We'll think about that tomorrow." I headed toward the steps. "Time to brush teeth. Let's get going." The two followed, sorta singing Frosty and Jingle Bells all mixed up. Jammies, brushings, and kisses later, I went down to the kitchen, pulled closed the swinging door, and began my Mickey Mouse inspired plan.

Chapter Twelve

Each evening, after tucking in sleepy children, I retrieved my project from the side yard. Remembering what Clarence, the choir director, told me about his wife's wreath making skills, I'd gone to McCrory's and bought craft wire right after that horrible night at practice. The Wilkinsons left several old, worn-out brooms in a back yard garage built before cars got bigger, or families drove two. I couldn't have parked one in it if I tried, but it did work as a shed. I picked the oldest broom and cut off the stick. My dad'd given me a starter tool kit, scrabbled from his work bench. Concord Presbyterian Church gave me the rest.

I went out back and, thank goodness, most of the pine branches I brought home three weeks ago were still somewhat fresh. Mom's advice about heat and sap was right on. The cold outside had done its job. With newspapers spread on the floor to help with the mess, I started, making up the construction plans as I went along.

Positioning the broom in the middle of the papers, I started laying out cut boughs in semblance of a two-dimensional tree, using the stick as trunk. Fitting branches flat to the center, I realized that this thing I was working on was taking on the image of Annie's hand trees that were covering Grindle.

"Gosh, this might be OK," I muttered to myself. "Now all that's left is to hook 'em together." I started at the bottom and wrapped around, through, and over the branches. After about a foot of fancy wire weaving, I lifted the stick to admire my creative genius. Every last branch fell. Damn, I'd forgotten about the stick. The children did not hear me swear.

Starting all over again, this time I used my daddy's handy dandy wire cutters and wrapped each branch separately, leaving a long tail at the end like I'd seen on the supports florists do with their flimsy flowers. Using the wire tails, I wrapped the broomstick, twisting each wire tight. Tada! That night I made my own hand print tree out of an old broom, church pines and less than a dollar's worth of wire. Back outside it went, hidden under the pile of leaves I never got bagged in the fall. Newspaper pages full of loose needles were stuffed in the trash, leaving the kitchen smelling of a tiny bit of hope.

***

"**M**ommeee."

I learned after Annie was born that there was no such thing as alone time. As soon as she started sleeping through the night, I would grab as much rest as possible so that I could get up extra early for quiet coffee time. And then along came Bobby. My round-eyed pile of curiosity loved nights more than hootie owls. He was fourteen months old before he realized that he wasn't starving to death at two-thirty in the morning. Finally, I could sleep enough to get back to my morning ritual of coffee and the Daily News.

"Mommeee, we gotta go to the store." There she stood in her Holly Hobbie nightgown, long blond hair wild around her head, all ready to start her day. It was 6:15 AM. My cup hadn't had enough time to cool off, let alone get half finished.

"Good grief, child, do you know what time it is?" *Stupid question.*

"Silly Mommy, of course I do. *You do? When did you learn to tell time?* It's time to go buy carrots."

"What? Good Lord, look outside. It's still dark. You go back to bed, young lady. Do not wake your brother. I will get you up when the sun gets up."

"But…"

"No buts. Now scoot." I deliberately kept my eyes to the paper, ignoring her. Finally, she disappeared. After a long swallow of my almost just right coffee, I started to think about their stockings. I'd saved enough to spend about ten dollars on each kid and with careful shopping, had stuff hidden in the bedroom window seat to fill two of my knee socks. Mom and Dad were having Christmas breakfast, so that took care of present opening. I knew their tree would be loaded.

After another cuppa and the day's funnies, I went upstairs. I found both of them zonked in Annie's bed, covered with all of their stuffed animals. I quietly went to my own room and snuggled under Aunt Emma's quilts. No school today. Carrots could wait.

That night I finished my four-foot-high, wired together, floppy tree. It looked kinda real...if you stood in the next county and squinted. Then reality hit. That flat thing would never stand up. Christmas was a blink away, and everything was ruined. Leaving it on the kitchen floor, I wandered into the playroom, sinking into the loveseat. Grindle, the paper decorated house plant, sat in front of me. I spoke to the Christmas Dog Bush.

"Well, you giant thing, you win. I can't make a Christmas tree no matter how hard I've tried. You are now our..." Then I noticed it. I jumped up, grabbed the little bit of craft wire I had left. A loop here, a twist there, and it was done. Back out to the leaf pile, and I went to bed and to the deepest sleep I'd had in a very long time.

Chapter Thirteen

The next day, Christmas Eve, was spent with a house full of happy baking elves, preparing for Santa. Early in the day I tuned in the local radio station that had started the carols the day after Thanksgiving. I hadn't felt the spirit until yesterday, and now the music was a wonderful addition to our baking fun.

"All I want for Christmas is my two front teeth, my two front teeth." Annie sang her heart out, having recently lost one of hers.

"Lissen Mommy. Caw Caw's comin' ta town." *My goodness that child sure is learning to talk.*

"Rum pa pum pum," we all sang together.

I measured, Annie mixed, and Bobby smooshed the gooey balls I rolled. They ate more raw dough than they should, but I didn't care, enjoying my own fair share. We all sprinkled red and green crystals on the cookies that actually got baked and that Annie frosted. I handled the little multi-colored balls, trying to control table roll off.

I must say that the three of us were as decorated as fancy as some of the cookies. Bobby was very good at finger licking, and Annie, well, I just couldn't figure out how she could eat so many candy eyes without getting all googly herself.

"Are these for Santa? I want to give him the prettiest ones." Annie started picking out what she considered the cookie cream of the crop.

"Absolutely, just make sure he gets the ones with the best decorations. I think he likes the kind with all the different colors." *I was sure Santa would enjoy those cookies...with her early morning coffee.*

Annie paused in her cookie sorting. "Can we take some to church tonight to give Mom Mom for her Santa plate?"

I smiled. "Fantastic idea! Let's bag up the very same kind with sprinkles that we're giving Santa. That way Santa will know that we are all family." *And Daddy will have them eaten before they get in the house.*

"Uh, oh, Mommy, I just thought of something."

"What is it, girl child?"

She shook her head. "We don't have a Santa's plate. We don't have any extra plates at all. What are we gonna do?"

"Um, we can take a paper towel and you can draw a circle and color it. We can use it as a pretend plate. How does that sound?" *I wasn't about to mention that half the dishes were in North Carolina, doing no good what so ever.*

"I like pretend, but a make-believe plate is kinda silly."

"That's true," I agreed. "But a paper plate is better than no plate."

"Mommy, I just thought of something else."

"What is it *this* time?" The cookie activity was almost over and there was a lot of cleaning up to do.

"Bobby 'n' me have little feet."

Mr. Sprinkle Licker looked up from his duties at the mention of his name. "And..." Gathering up the mixing bowl and utensils, I headed to the sink.

"And I can't figure out how Santa can put anything in our socks." She frowned. "What're we gonna do?"

Ah, I had an answer for that one. "Would you guys like to borrow a pair of my knee socks? I have a set in my sock drawer."

"My Caw Caus socks too small? No presents?"

Annie smiled. "It's ok. Mommy's got big feet."

By four o'clock we'd downed peanut butter sandwiches and were sporting scrubbed hands and faces. Christmas Eve services were at six thirty, and Mom reminded me that the choir always sings their holiday Cantata first, so we'd better be there by five fifteen. Annie had a beautiful red velvet dress from the Goodwill, and I was lucky enough to find Bobby a cute plaid vest with built-in bow tie. I wore the outfit from last year when my world was falling apart, a matching plaid skirt and fringed shawl set.

Once the kids were settled in the nursery and properly supervised, I joined my parents. This service, unlike the last one, left me peaceful. All of next day plans were settled. I knew the morning would be fine. This time tears during the Silent Night candle lighting were brought on by the beauty of the Season and not because of fears and regrets. These tears were filled with joy.

Chapter Fourteen

"Pop Pop, look." Annie was the first to notice, pulling her grandfather past Christmas treats, two hand-shaking ministers, and an eighteenth century costumed brass quartet, out into falling snow. Grass was barely covered, but that didn't matter. It was magical just the same.

Daddy scooped her up. "Watch this." He stuck out his tongue and caught a flake. "You do it."

By the time I was past the preachers and into the night, I found my father and daughter, their snow catchers fast at work. Mom and Bobby were waylaid at the punch and cookie table. The tuba player puffed his cheeks and blew 'boom ba bum be boom ba boom', opening notes of "Here We Come a Wassailing" several times, announcing refreshments. To Mom's astonishment, Bobby answered the notes perfectly, his little boy voice making almost cherubic tuba sounds.

"Looks like you know music," observed the trumpet player standing close by.

"Uh, huh, Caw Caus comin' to town," came the sing-song reply. "Betta watch out, betta not cry…"

Mom stuck a cookie in his mouth. "Betta find Pop Pop." Nodding to the musicians and the ministers, she escorted him out the front door and into our first snowfall of the season.

"Caw Caus snow," whispered the wide eyed child. "Caw Caus comin' to town." Looking skyward, his face fell. "No red nose so bright, no Rudolph sleigh tonight." His tears started, prompting Annie's sniffles, too.

Mother saved the day, er, night. Scooping him up, she pointed to a transmission tower about a mile away that was blinking, warning low flying airplanes. "Look everybody, look. I see a red light. Could it be reindeer?"

The adults turned, following Mom Mom's lead. The light was far away enough to be barely distinguishable, and that was perfect for the spinning of the red nosed tale.

"Mother," I said with a wide-eyed smile, "I think you're right. Could Santa be flying already? Isn't too early?"

Annie got a snuggle from her Pop Pop. "It's never too early to believe," he said. "I do. How about you, Little Missy?"

She wiggled deeper into his arms. "I believe in Santa. Mrs. Cunningham read us a book about not a creature was stirring, not even a house." She looked up at him, eyes serious. "Pop Pop, how can a house stir? Can a house make cookies like we did? That would take a really big spoon."

Mother and I exchanged giggly looks, but kept quiet, the moment too precious to interfere.

"Yes, ma'am, it would. However this stirring means to move around and the story says not a creature was stirring, not even a mouse, not a house." He shook his head, tone dramatic. "I know for a fact that there is not a mouse in your house, just your mommy, you guys, and a monkey. That's enough creatures."

"Yes, that's enough creatures." The snow was getting thicker and I could see that the salt and cinder trucks hadn't made their pass. "Mom, Dad, we need to hit the road. Smithfield Street could be slick." I smiled. "We have stockings to hang, you know."

Daddy kissed his Little Missy's cheek and handed her over to me.

"Oomph, girl, down you go. You're getting to big for me to carry." Hugging my parents goodbye and grabbing children's hands, we walked through the church parking lot, tongues out to catch all we could.

The thought of wrecking on this snowy Christmas Eve really scared me. As we slowly rolled through the blinking yellow caution light controlling traffic at the intersection of Smithfield and Lincoln Avenue, I saw police at the bottom of the hill, ambulance already there. Silently praying for all, I tightly gripped the wheel. However, thank heavens, our careful drive home was uneventful, save a little skid as I turned onto Daily Street. When I parked in front of our house and looked in the backseat, my heart swelled. Both children had fallen asleep holding hands.

"Come on, you guys," I gently jostled them. "Come on; stir your bones."

Annie's eyes opened. "Christmas?" She looked around, not registering her surroundings.

"Almost. Christmas Eve. Wake your brother. We need to go in the house, hang stockings, and get to bed so that Christmas Day can come." The three of us made footprints on the snowy front porch steps.

Once inside and dusted off, I sat back and watched Annie take over. She scurried up the steps and I could hear her in my dresser. Back down she flew with the itchy socks I'd attempted to knit many years ago and couldn't stand to wear. However, since they were my first attempt at yarn work, in the drawer they stayed.

Lifting each child, they snagged the wool on those left behind cup hooks.

"Uh, oh, Mommy."

"What, child? What's the 'uh-oh' about? Things look good to me."

"Mommy, are you on the naughty list? You didn't hang a stocking."

Oh, crap, how do I handle this one?

"And Zippy needs a stocking, too." She looked to her brother for advice. "Mommy 'n' Zippy are not gonna get presents. What are we going to do?"

Bobby pondered this dilemma, and then giggled. "Mommy's got unnerpants socks. Two socks. One for Mommy and one for Zippy."

Oh, good grief, he's talking about panty hose. Never thought they paid attention when I stripped off those suckers every day after school.

Another quick trip to my dresser and all problems solved. Annie brought out her paper towel masterpiece and treats, reverently placing cookies, carrots, and milk offerings on the hearth. Our fireplace was resplendent with two stockings, a pair of pantyhose, and a pretend plate full of goodies.

Holding hands, me softly singing 'It Came Upon a Midnight Clear', we climbed the steps to bed, me promising to unlock the front door. As soon as the sleepy heads were settled in, I tiptoed back down to work that wonderful magic called a Parent's Christmas Eve.

The last thing I remembered as I fell asleep was a distinct thud on the roof. Could it be?

Chapter Fifteen

Rinsing my coffee cup, wiping off all traces of multicolored evidence from the rim, I stomped up to their rooms hoping to raise such a clatter. "HO! HO! HO! Merry Christmas!" I couldn't contain myself. Scooping up Bobby, we marched down the steps singing 'We Wish You a Merry Christmas'. By the fire place were half-eaten carrots, empty milk glass, and cookie crumbs scattered on the hearth. The paper towel plate was crumpled with traces of sprinkles like lipstick on a napkin. The hung knee socks and hosiery were missing.

Bobby started to cry. "Socks gone. No Caw Caus, no Caw Caus tree." Annie joined him, tears streaming.

"Hold on, you two. Stop that stuff right now." I had to get them away from the fireplace. "Of course, Santa was here. Look at the carrot, the crumbs. Maybe he moved the stockings." I headed toward my handy work in the playroom. "Let's go to the kitchen and see if Santa poured some more milk." They dragged behind me until...

"Mommy, Mommy look what Grindle brought."

Grindle?

"Lookie, lookie, Grindle brought us a Christmas tree. She put it on the sock sorter hook!" Annie started clapping, jumping for joy. Attached to that long ignored plant bracket was a wired together, church pines, stick in the middle, flat Christmas tree. The stapled green, hand shaped, red fingernail garland that used to adorn the giant Christmas Dog Bush, were now on the tree. Filled stockings lay below it, obviously magically moved from hearth to window seat by the fat man himself.

"Mommy, Mommy, Caw Caus came. Caw Caus came." Bobby grabbed his stocking, hugging it like a baby. "Can I look inside?"

Annie stood in front of the window seat, studying my handy work. "Yep, it wouldn't have made it down our chimney."

"You wanna go check the front door? It's been unlocked all night." I waited.

"Mommee, Mommee, there's deer prints on the front porch."

Deer prints? I'd made boot prints in the snow. "Let's see." Sure enough, some sort of animal had walked across our front porch, leaving four footed tracks beside the imprints I'd made. *Thank you, stray*

whatever, for the icing on this magical cake.
"Wowee kazowee," was all I said.

"Kowzee," Bobby echoed, still hugging his sock.

"Come on, you guys, let's see what we got."

I softly cried as I watched my beloved children have their first Christmas as a new family. At that moment I knew we were OK. No matter what was coming, we could make it. The promise of the day shined in all our eyes. Thank you, broomstick Christmas tree, for the best day in the whole wide world.

Oh, and thank you Grindle, the Christmas Dog Bush. Too bad I didn't buy you a present. Maybe next year.

THE END

About Jacqueline T. Moore

Jacqueline T. Moore works and plays in Myrtle Beach, South Carolina. She says. "Living in the south makes me a sunflower…and a beach bum!" As a writer and educator, Jacqueline surrounds herself with words. She savors the sounds and sense of letters put together to create a lasting memory. THE BROOMSTICK CHRISTMAS TREE is just that, lasting memories.

Jacqueline is also the author of the popular historical trilogy THE CANARY, THE CHECKERBOARD, and THE CORNERPOST accompanied by THE CANARY COMPANION COOKBOOK. She also is the author of the Christmas e-short story SAY HI FOR ME.

Visit her at www.jacqueline-t-moore.com, on Facebook @Jacqueline T. Moore, and on Instagram @Jacqueline. T. Moore for conversations and updates.

Social Media

Facebook:

https://www.facebook.com/pages/Jacqueline
-T-Moore/4765684196045
Website:
www.jacqueline-t-moore.com
Instagram:
https://www.instagram.com/jacqueline.t.mo
ore
Email:
Jacqueline@jacqueline-t-moore.com

Acknowledgements

With much appreciation I thank Georgene Jacobs, Julie Jacobs, Uta Andrews, and Ellen 'Cookie' Brenner for their very valuable conversations and input. I also thank Robert Freit for giving me the best piece of advice I'd heard in a really long time.

The Broomstick Christmas Tree Recipes

Pop Pop's French Coffee

2 kitchen mugs of hot morning coffee
Milk straight from the fridge
Tabletop sugar bowl
2 teaspoons for stirring

Fill two kitchen mugs half full of coffee. Top off with cold milk. Give one mug to a child. Measure out sugar (3-4 spoonsful) into mugs. Allow child to stir and enjoy with Mom Mom's cinnamon strudel coffee cake.

Mom Mom's Cinnamon Strudel (Streusel) Coffee Cake

CAKE
Beat together
2/3 c soft butter
½ c sugar
2 eggs
Add alternating dry and wet ingredients
1 ½ c flour
1 ½ tsp baking powder
½ c milk
Add in

1 tsp vanilla
2 tbs sour cream

STREUSEL

Cut in
2 tbs cold butter
1 c brown sugar
1tbs cinnamon

Stir in
1c chopped nuts
1c raisins

Put ½ of the batter in a buttered 8x8 pan. Layer with ½ streusel mix. Add rest of batter and crumble rest of streusel mix on top. Bake 350 degrees for about 45 minutes.

Mom Mom's Freezer Vegetable Soup

All leftover dinner vegetables and cooked meat from the last month or so are stored in one large freezer container. After each contribution, return the container to the freezer. When the container is filled, it's time to make soup.

Put 1 to 2 cups hot water in a crockpot. Dump frozen leftovers in water. Set the crockpot on 'high' for four hours. Stir vegetables in broth. Taste and add salt, pepper, and other spices of your choice. Mom Mom used bay leaves and allspice berries. Lower the crock pot temperature to 'low'. Allow soup to simmer another 4 hours or until the aroma makes you so hungry you can't leave it alone.

Mom always served the soup with Jiffy Mix cornbread.

Annie's Macky Cheese

1 cup elbow macaroni
1/3 cup powdered milk
1 inch cut Velveeta processed cheese, cubed
Salt and pepper
Yellow food coloring

Boil 4 cups salted water. Stir in 1 cup of elbows. Cook 7-8 minutes. Drain, saving a cup of the macaroni water. Add 1/3 cup powdered milk to the water and stir until it is dissolved. Add enough drops of food coloring to milk mixture to make it very yellow. Add milk and cubed cheese to hot macaroni. Stir until the Velveeta is melted and the macaroni looks like it is covered with cheese. Serve.

Thanksgiving Cranberry Grind-up

1 bag fresh cranberries
3 oranges cut into eights
1 c sugar
1 c halved pecans

Process the cranberries and oranges using a tabletop food grinder. Mix well in a large bowl. Add the sugar and stir until the fruits seem juicier. Cover and refrigerate overnight. Right before time to eat, fold in the nuts. Serve.

Christmas Sugar Cookies

Cream together
1 1/3 c soften butter
1 ½ c sugar
2 tsp vanilla

Add
2 eggs

Beat until fluffy

Stir in
¼ c milk

Sift
4 c flour

1 tbs baking powder
½ tsp salt

Thoroughly mix with wet ingredients.
Chill one hour.

Roll out dough on floured surface until ¼ inch thick to be cut with shaped cookie cutters *or* give tablespoons of dough to children to roll into balls and smoosh on floured surface.

Bake on greased cookie sheet at 375 degrees for 6-8 minutes. Cool slightly and remove from pan. Add icing if you want or just turn the kids loose with shakers of colorful sugar sprinkles. Serve to Santa.

The Broomstick Christmas Tree Book Club Guidelines

1. The Broomstick Christmas Tree is a story of a new life crafted out of necessity. Have you ever had to make something happen when you had next to nothing? What was it? Were you proud of your outcome?

2. Susan was a young wife and mother during a time of severe social change and upheaval. Example: She was expected to wear white gloves to church; husbands had all the financial credit; the seating at the family Thanksgiving table spoke volumes. Think about the times when you were brave enough to go against the norm. What did you do? Were you successful?

3. Susan realized that her husband, Danny, was a product of his upbringing, could not change, and felt she had to get away to give her children a different life.

Do you think this was a wise move or a mistake? Why?

4. The children, Annie and Bobby, displayed some early talents. Just for fun project what they will be when they are adults. Explain.

5. The desolate Christmas Eve scene in the bar is great contrast to the cookie scene the next year. What other things do you think will change as time passes?